# SECOND CHILDHOOD

# SECOND CHILDHOOD

by Clifford D. Simak

You did not die.

There was no normal way to die.

You lived as carelessly and as recklessly as you could and you hoped that you would be lucky and be accidentally killed.

You kept on living and you got tired of living.

"God, how tired a man can get of living!" Andrew Young said.

John Riggs, chairman of the immortality commission, cleared his throat.

"You realize," he said to Andrew Young, "that this petition is a highly irregular procedure to bring to our attention."

He picked up the sheaf of papers off the table and ruffled through them rapidly.

"There is no precedent," he added.

"I had hoped," said Andrew Young, "to establish precedent."

Commissioner Stanford said, "I must admit that you have made a good case, Ancestor Young. Yet you must realize that this commission has no possible jurisdiction over the life of any person, except to see that everyone is assured of all the benefits of immortality and to work out any kinks that may show up."

"I am well aware of that," answered Young, "and it seems to me that my case is one of the kinks you mention."

He stood silently, watching the faces of the members of the board. They are afraid, he thought. Every one of them. Afraid of the day they will face the thing I am facing now. They have sought an answer and there is no answer yet except the pitifully basic answer, the brutally fundamental answer that I have given them.

"My request is simple," he told them, calmly. "I have asked for permission to discontinue life. And since suicide has been made psychologically impossible, I have asked that this commission appoint a panel of next-friends to make the necessary and somewhat distasteful arrangements to bring about the discontinuance of my life."

"If we did," said Riggs, "we would destroy everything we have. There is no virtue in a life of only five thousand years. No more than in a life of only a hundred years. If Man is to be immortal, he must be genuinely immortal. He cannot compromise."

"And yet," said Young, "my friends are gone."

*

He gestured at the papers Riggs held in his hands. "I have them listed there," he said. "Their names and when and where and how they died. Take a look at them. More than two hundred names. People of my own generation and of the generations closely following mine. Their names and the photo-copies of their death certificates."

He put both of his hands upon the table, palms flat against the table, and leaned his weight upon his arms.

"Take a look at how they died," he said. "Every one involves accidental violence. Some of them drove their vehicles too fast and, more than likely, very recklessly. One fell off a cliff when he reached down to pick a flower that was growing on its edge. A case of deliberately poor judgment, to my mind. One got stinking drunk and took a bath and passed out in the tub. He drowned...."

"Ancestor Young," Riggs said sharply, "you are surely not implying these folks were suicides."

"No," Andrew Young said bitterly. "We abolished suicide three thousand years ago, cleared it clean out of human minds. How could they have killed themselves?"

Stanford said, peering up at Young, "I believe, sir, you sat on the board that resolved that problem."

Andrew Young nodded. "It was after the first wave of suicides. I remember it quite well. It took years of work. We had to change human perspective, shift certain facets of human nature. We had to condition human reasoning by education and propaganda and instill a new set of moral values. I think we did a good job of it. Perhaps too good a job. Today a man can no more think of deliberately committing suicide than he could think of overthrowing our government. The very idea, the very word is repulsive, instinctively repulsive. You can come a long way, gentlemen, in three thousand years."

He leaned across the table and tapped the sheaf of papers with a lean, tense finger.

"They didn't kill themselves," he said. "They did not commit suicide. They just didn't give a damn. They were tired of living ... as I am tired of living. So they lived recklessly in every way. Perhaps there always was a secret hope that they would drown while drunk or their car would hit a tree or...."

*

He straightened up and faced them. "Gentlemen," he said. "I am 5,786 years of age. I was born at Lancaster, Maine, on the planet Earth on September 21, 1968. I have served humankind well in those fifty-seven centuries. My record is there for you to see. Boards, commissions, legislative posts, diplomatic missions. No one can say that I have shirked my duty. I submit that I have paid any debt I owe humanity ... even the well-intentioned debt for a chance at immortality."

"We wish," said Riggs, "that you would reconsider."

"I am a lonely man," replied Young. "A lonely man and tired. I have no friends. There is nothing any longer that holds my interest. It is my hope that I can make you see the desirability of assuming jurisdiction in cases such as mine. Someday you may find a solution to the problem, but until that time arrives, I ask you, in the name of mercy, to give us relief from life."

"The problem, as we see it," said Riggs, "is to find some way to wipe out mental perspective. When a man lives as you have, sir, for fifty centuries, he has too long a memory. The memories add up to the disadvantage of present realities and prospects for the future."

"I know," said Young. "I remember we used to talk about that in the early days. It was one of the problems which was recognized when immortality first became practical. But we always thought that memory would erase itself, that the brain could accommodate only so many memories, that when it got full up it would dump the old ones. It hasn't worked that way."

He made a savage gesture. "Gentlemen, I can recall my childhood much more vividly than I recall anything that happened yesterday."

"Memories are buried," said Riggs, "and in the old days, when men lived no longer than a hundred years at most, it was thought those buried memories were forgotten. Life, Man told himself, is a process of forgetting. So Man wasn't too worried over memories when he became immortal. He thought he would forget them."

"He should have known," argued Young. "I can remember my father, and I remember him much more intimately than I will remember you gentlemen once I leave this room.... I can remember my father telling me that, in his later years, he could recall things which happened in his childhood that had been forgotten all his younger years. And that, alone, should have tipped us off. The brain buries only the newer memories deeply ... they are not available; they do not rise to bother one, because they are not sorted or oriented or correlated or whatever it is that the brain may do with them. But once they are all nicely docketed and filed, they pop up in an instant."

\*

Riggs nodded agreement. "There's a lag of a good many years in the brain's bookkeeping. We will overcome it in time."

"We have tried," said Stanford. "We tried conditioning, the same solution that worked with suicides. But in this, it didn't work. For a man's life is built upon his memories. There are certain basic memories that must remain intact. With conditioning, you could not be selective. You could not keep the structural memories and winnow out the trash. It didn't work that way."

"There was one machine that worked," Riggs put in. "It got rid of memories. I don't understand exactly how it worked, but it did the job all right. It did too good a job. It swept the mind as clean as an empty room. It didn't leave a thing. It took all memories and it left no capacity to build a new set. A man went in a human being and came out a vegetable."

"Suspended animation," said Stanford, "would be a solution. If we had suspended animation. Simply stack a man away until we found the answer, then revive and recondition him."

"Be that as it may," Young told them, "I should like your most earnest consideration of my petition. I do not feel quite equal to waiting until you have the answer solved."

Riggs said, harshly, "You are asking us to legalize death."

Young nodded. "If you wish to phrase it that way. I'm asking it in the name of common decency."

Commissioner Stanford said, "We can ill afford to lose you, Ancestor."

Young sighed. "There is that damned attitude again. Immortality pays all debts. When a man is made immortal, he has received full compensation for everything that he may endure. I have lived longer than any man could be expected to live and still I am denied the dignity of old age. A man's desires are few, and quickly sated, and yet he is expected to continue living with desires burned up and blown away to ash. He gets to a point where nothing has a value ... even to a point where his own personal values are no more than shadows. Gentlemen, there was a time when I could not have committed murder ... literally could not have forced myself to kill another man ... but today I could, without a second thought. Disillusion and cynicism have crept in upon me and I have no conscience."

*

"There are compensations," Riggs said. "Your family...."

"They get in my hair," said Young disgustedly. "Thousands upon thousands of young squirts calling me Grandsire and Ancestor and coming to me for advice they practically never follow. I don't know even a fraction of them and I listen to them carefully explain a relationship so tangled and trivial that it makes me yawn in their faces. It's all new to them and so old, so damned and damnably old to me."

"Ancestor Young," said Stanford, "you have seen Man spread out from Earth to distant stellar systems. You have seen the human race expand from one planet to several thousand planets. You have had a part in this. Is there not some satisfaction...."

"You're talking in abstracts," Young cut in. "What I am concerned about is myself ... a certain specific mass of protoplasm shaped in biped form and tagged by the designation, ironic as it may seem, of Andrew Young. I have been unselfish all my life. I've asked little for myself. Now I am being utterly and entirely selfish and I ask that this matter be regarded as a personal problem rather than as a racial abstraction."

"Whether you'll admit it or not," said Stanford, "it is more than a personal problem. It is a problem which some day must be solved for the salvation of the race."

"That is what I am trying to impress upon you," Young snapped. "It is a problem that you must face. Some day you will solve it, but until you do, you must make provisions for those who face the unsolved problem."

"Wait a while," counseled Chairman Riggs. "Who knows? Today, tomorrow."

"Or a million years from now," Young told him bitterly and left, a tall, vigorous-looking man whose step was swift in anger where normally it was slow with weariness and despair.

\*

There was yet a chance, of course.

But there was little hope.

How can a man go back almost six thousand years and snare a thing he never understood?

And yet Andrew Young remembered it. Remembered it as clearly as if it had been a thing that had happened in the morning of this very day.

# CLIFFORD D. SIMAK

It was a shining thing, a bright thing, a happiness that was brand-new and fresh as a bluebird's wing of an April morning or a shy woods flower after sudden rain.

He had been a boy and he had seen the bluebird and he had no words to say the thing he felt, but he had held up his tiny fingers and pointed and shaped his lips to coo.

Once, he thought, I had it in my very fingers and I did not have the experience to know what it was, nor the value of it. And now I know the value, but it has escaped me—it escaped me on the day that I began to think like a human being. The first adult thought pushed it just a little and the next one pushed it farther and finally it was gone entirely and I didn't even know that it had gone.

He sat in the chair on the flagstone patio and felt the Sun upon him, filtering through the branches of trees misty with the breaking leaves of Spring.

Something else, thought Andrew Young. Something that was not human—yet. A tiny animal that had many ways to choose, many roads to walk. And, of course, I chose the wrong way. I chose the human way. But there was another way. I know there must have been. A fairy way—or a brownie way, or maybe even pixie. That sounds foolish and childish now, but it wasn't always.

I chose the human way because I was guided into it. I was pushed and shoved, like a herded sheep.

I grew up and I lost the thing I held.

He sat and made his mind go hard and tried to analyze what it was he sought and there was no name for it. Except happiness. And happiness was a state of being, not a thing to regain and grasp.

*

But he could remember how it felt. With his eyes open in the present, he could remember the brightness of the day of the past, the clean-washed goodness of it, the wonder of the colors that were more brilliant than he ever since had seen—as if it were the first second after Creation and the world was still shiningly new.

# SECOND CHILDHOOD

It was that new, of course. It would be that new to a child.

But that didn't explain it all.

It didn't explain the bottomless capacity for seeing and knowing and believing in the beauty and the goodness of a clean new world. It didn't explain the almost non-human elation of knowing that there were colors to see and scents to smell and soft green grass to touch.

I'm insane, Andrew Young said to himself. Insane, or going insane. But if insanity will take me back to an understanding of the strange perception I had when I was a child, and lost, I'll take insanity.

He leaned back in his chair and let his eyes go shut and his mind drift back.

He was crouching in a corner of a garden and the leaves were drifting down from the walnut trees like a rain of saffron gold. He lifted one of the leaves and it slipped from his fingers, for his hands were chubby still and not too sure in grasping. But he tried again and he clutched it by the stem in one stubby fist and he saw that it was not just a blob of yellowness, but delicate, with many little veins. When he held it so that the Sun struck it, he imagined that he could almost see through it, the gold was spun so fine.

He crouched with the leaf clutched tightly in his hand and for a moment there was a silence that held him motionless. Then he heard the frost-loosened leaves pattering all around him, pattering as they fell, talking in little whispers as they sailed down through the air and found themselves a bed with their golden fellows.

In that moment he knew that he was one with the leaves and the whispers that they made, one with the gold and the autumn sunshine and the far blue mist upon the hill above the apple orchard.

A foot crunched stone behind him and his eyes came open and the golden leaves were gone.

"I am sorry if I disturbed you, Ancestor," said the man. "I had an appointment for this hour, but I would not have disturbed you if I had known."

Young stared at him reproachfully without answering.

"I am kin," the man told him.

"I wouldn't doubt it," said Andrew Young. "The Galaxy is cluttered up with descendants of mine."

The man was very humble. "Of course, you must resent us sometimes. But we are proud of you, sir. I might almost say that we revere you. No other family—"

"I know," interrupted Andrew Young. "No other family has any fossil quite so old as I am."

"Nor as wise," said the man.

Andrew Young snorted. "Cut out that nonsense. Let's hear what you have to say and get it over with."

\*

The technician was harassed and worried and very frankly puzzled. But he stayed respectful, for one always was respectful to an ancestor, whoever he might be. Today there were mighty few left who had been born into a mortal world.

Not that Andrew Young looked old. He looked like all adults, a fine figure of a person in the early twenties.

The technician shifted uneasily. "But, sir, this ... this...."

"Teddy bear," said Young.

"Yes, of course. An extinct terrestrial subspecies of animal?"

"It's a toy," Young told him. "A very ancient toy. All children used to have them five thousand years ago. They took them to bed."

\*

The technician shuddered. "A deplorable custom. Primitive."

"Depends on the viewpoint," said Young. "I've slept with them many a time. There's a world of comfort in one, I can personally assure you."

The technician saw that it was no use to argue. He might as well fabricate the thing and get it over with.

"I can build you a fine model, sir," he said, trying to work up some enthusiasm. "I'll build in a response mechanism so that it can give simple answers to certain keyed questions and, of course, I'll fix it so it'll walk, either on two legs or four...."

"No," said Andrew Young.

The technician looked surprised and hurt. "No?"

"No," repeated Andrew Young. "I don't want it fancied up. I want it a simple lump of make-believe. No wonder the children of today have no imagination. Modern toys entertain them with a bag of tricks that leave the young'uns no room for imagination. They couldn't possibly think up, on their own, all the screwy things these new toys do. Built-in responses and implied consciousness and all such mechanical trivia...."

"You just want a stuffed fabric," said the technician, sadly, "with jointed arms and legs."

"Precisely," agreed Young.

"You're sure you want fabric, sir? I could do a neater job in plastics."

"Fabric," Young insisted firmly, "and it must be scratchy."

"Scratchy, sir?"

"Sure. You know. Bristly. So it scratches when you rub your face against it."

"But no one in his right mind would want to rub his face...."

"I would," said Andrew Young. "I fully intend to do so."

"As you wish, sir," the technician answered, beaten now.

"When you get it done," said Young, "I have some other things in mind."

"Other things?" The technician looked wildly about, as if seeking some escape.

"A high chair," said Young. "And a crib. And a woolly dog. And buttons."

"Buttons?" asked the technician. "What are buttons?"

"I'll explain it all to you," Young told him airily. "It all is very simple."

*

# CLIFFORD D. SIMAK

It seemed, when Andrew Young came into the room, that Riggs and Stanford had been expecting him, had known that he was coming and had been waiting for him.

He wasted no time on preliminaries or formalities.

They know, he told himself. They know, or they have guessed. They would be watching me. Ever since I brought in my petition, they have been watching me, wondering what I would be thinking, trying to puzzle out what I might do next. They know every move I've made, they know about the toys and the furniture and all the other things. And I don't need to tell them what I plan to do.

"I need some help," he said, and they nodded soberly, as if they had guessed he needed help.

"I want to build a house," he explained. "A big house. Much larger than the usual house."

Riggs said, "We'll draw the plans for you. Do anything else that you—"

"A house," Young went on, "about four or five times as big as the ordinary house. Four or five times normal scale, I mean. Doors twenty-five to thirty feet high and everything else in proportion."

"Neighbors or privacy?" asked Stanford.

"Privacy," said Young.

"We'll take care of it," promised Riggs. "Leave the matter of the house to us."

Young stood for a long moment, looking at the two of them. Then he said, "I thank you, gentlemen. I thank you for your helpfulness and your understanding. But most of all I thank you for not asking any questions."

He turned slowly and walked out of the room and they sat in silence for minutes after he was gone.

Finally, Stanford offered a deduction: "It will have to be a place that a boy would like. Woods to run in and a little stream to fish in and a field where he can fly his kites. What else could it be?"

"He's been out ordering children's furniture and toys," Riggs agreed. "Stuff from five thousand years ago. The kind of things he used when he was a child. But scaled to adult size."

"Now," said Stanford, "he wants a house built to the same proportions. A house that will make him think or help him believe that he is a child. But will it work, Riggs? His body will not change. He cannot make it change. It will only be in his mind."

"Illusion," declared Riggs. "The illusion of bigness in relation to himself. To a child, creeping on the floor, a door is twenty-five to thirty feet high, relatively. Of course the child doesn't know that. But Andrew Young does. I don't see how he'll overcome that."

"At first," suggested Stanford, "he will know that it's illusion, but after a time, isn't there a possibility that it will become reality so far as he's concerned? That's why he needs our help. So that the house will not be firmly planted in his memory as a thing that's merely out of proportion ... so that it will slide from illusion into reality without too great a strain."

"We must keep our mouths shut." Riggs nodded soberly. "There must be no interference. It's a thing he must do himself ... entirely by himself. Our help with the house must be the help of an unseen, silent agency. Like brownies, I think the term was that he used, we must help and be never seen. Intrusion by anyone would introduce a jarring note and would destroy illusion and that is all he has to work on. Illusion pure and simple."

"Others have tried," objected Stanford, pessimistic again. "Many others. With gadgets and machines...."

"None has tried it," said Riggs, "with the power of mind alone. With the sheer determination to wipe out five thousand years of memory."

"That will be his stumbling block," said Stanford. "The old, dead memories are the things he has to beat. He has to get rid of them ... not just bury them, but get rid of them for good and all, forever."

"He must do more than that," said Riggs. "He must replace his memories with the outlook he had when he was a child. His mind must be washed out, refreshed, wiped clean and shining and made new again ... ready to live another five thousand years."

The two men sat and looked at one another and in each other's eyes they saw a single thought—the day would come when they, too, each of them alone, would face the problem Andrew Young faced.

"We must help," said Riggs, "in every way we can and we must keep watch and we must be ready ... but Andrew Young cannot know that we are helping or that we are watching him. We must anticipate the materials and tools and the aids that he may need."

\*

Stanford started to speak, then hesitated, as if seeking in his mind for the proper words.

"Yes," said Riggs. "What is it?"

"Later on," Stanford managed to say, "much later on, toward the very end, there is a certain factor that we must supply. The one thing that he will need the most and the one thing that he cannot think about, even in advance. All the rest can be stage setting and he can still go on toward the time when it becomes reality. All the rest may be make-believe, but one thing must come as genuine or the entire effort will collapse in failure."

Riggs nodded. "Of course. That's something we'll have to work out carefully."

"If we can," Stanford said.

\*

The yellow button over here and the red one over there and the green one doesn't fit, so I'll throw it on the floor and just for the fun of it, I'll put the pink one in my mouth and someone will find me with it and they'll raise a ruckus because they will be afraid that I will swallow it.

And there's nothing, absolutely nothing, that I love better than a full-blown ruckus. Especially if it is over me.

# SECOND CHILDHOOD

"Ug," said Andrew Young, and he swallowed the button.

He sat stiff and straight in the towering high chair and then, in a fury, swept the oversized muffin tin and its freight of buttons crashing to the floor.

For a second he felt like weeping in utter frustration and then a sense of shame crept in on him.

Big baby, he said to himself.

Crazy to be sitting in an overgrown high chair, playing with buttons and mouthing baby talk and trying to force a mind conditioned by five thousand years of life into the channels of an infant's thoughts.

Carefully he disengaged the tray and slid it out, cautiously shinnied down the twelve-foot-high chair.

The room engulfed him, the ceiling towering far above him.

The neighbors, he told himself, no doubt thought him crazy, although none of them had said so. Come to think of it, he had not seen any of his neighbors for a long spell now.

A suspicion came into his mind. Maybe they knew what he was doing, maybe they were deliberately keeping out of his way in order not to embarrass him.

That, of course, would be what they would do if they had realized what he was about. But he had expected ... he had expected ... that fellow, what's his name? ... at the commission, what's the name of that commission, anyhow? Well, anyway, he'd expected a fellow whose name he couldn't remember from a commission the name of which he could not recall to come snooping around, wondering what he might be up to, offering to help, spoiling the whole setup, everything he'd planned.

I can't remember, he complained to himself. I can't remember the name of a man whose name I knew so short a time ago as yesterday. Nor the name of a commission that I knew as well as I know my name. I'm getting forgetful. I'm getting downright childish.

Childish?

Childish!

18

Childish and forgetful.

Good Lord, thought Andrew Young, that's just the way I want it.

On hands and knees he scrabbled about and picked up the buttons, put them in his pocket. Then, with the muffin tin underneath his arm, he shinnied up the high chair and, seating himself comfortably, sorted out the buttons in the pan.

The green one over here in this compartment and the yellow one ... oops, there she goes onto the floor. And the red one in with the blue one and this one ... this one ... what's the color of this one? Color? What's that?

What is what?

What—

*

"It's almost time," said Stanford, "and we are ready, as ready as we'll ever be. We'll move in when the time is right, but we can't move in too soon. Better to be a little late than a little early. We have all the things we need. Special size diapers and—"

"Good Lord," exclaimed Riggs, "it won't go that far, will it?"

"It should," said Stanford. "It should go even further to work right. He got lost yesterday. One of our men found him and led him home. He didn't have the slightest idea where he was and he was getting pretty scared and he cried a little. He chattered about birds and flowers and he insisted that our man stay and play with him."

Riggs chuckled softly. "Did he?"

"Oh, certainly. He came back worn to a frazzle."

"Food?" I asked Riggs. "How is he feeding himself?"

"We see there's a supply of stuff, cookies and such-wise, left on a low shelf, where he can get at them. One of the robots cooks up some more substantial stuff on a regular schedule and leaves it where he can find it. We have to be careful. We can't mess around too much. We can't intrude on him. I have a feeling he's almost reached an actual turning point. We can't afford to upset things now that he's come this far."

19

# SECOND CHILDHOOD

"The android's ready?"

"Just about," said Stanford.

"And the playmates?"

"Ready. They were less of a problem."

"There's nothing more that we can do?"

"Nothing," Stanford said. "Just wait, that's all. Young has carried himself this far by the sheer force of will alone. That will is gone now. He can't consciously force himself any further back. He is more child than adult now. He's built up a regressive momentum and the only question is whether that momentum is sufficient to carry him all the way back to actual babyhood."

"It has to go back to that?" Riggs looked unhappy, obviously thinking of his own future. "You're only guessing, aren't you?"

"All the way or it simply is no good," Stanford said dogmatically. "He has to get an absolutely fresh start. All the way or nothing."

"And if he gets stuck halfway between? Half child, half man, what then?"

"That's something I don't want to think about," Stanford said.

*

He had lost his favorite teddy bear and gone to hunt it in the dusk that was filled with elusive fireflies and the hush of a world quieting down for the time of sleep. The grass was drenched with dew and he felt the cold wetness of it soaking through his shoes as he went from bush to hedge to flowerbed, looking for the missing toy.

It was necessary, he told himself, that he find the nice little bear, for it was the one that slept with him and if he did not find it, he knew that it would spend a lonely and comfortless night. But at no time did he admit, even to his innermost thought, that it was he who needed the bear and not the bear who needed him.

A soaring bat swooped low and for a horrified moment, catching sight of the zooming terror, a blob of darkness in the gathering dusk, he squatted low against the ground, huddling against the sudden fear that came out of the night. Sounds of fright bubbled in his throat and

CLIFFORD D. SIMAK

now he saw the great dark garden as an unknown place, filled with
lurking shadows that lay in wait for him.

He stayed cowering against the ground and tried to fight off the
alien fear that growled from behind each bush and snarled in every
darkened corner. But even as the fear washed over him, there was
one hidden corner of his mind that knew there was no need of fear.
It was as if that one area of his brain still fought against the rest of
him, as if that small section of cells might know that the bat was no
more than a flying bat, that the shadows in the garden were no more
than absence of light.

There was a reason, he knew, why he should not be afraid—a good
reason born of a certain knowledge he no longer had. And that he
should have such knowledge seemed unbelievable, for he was scarcely
two years old.

*

He tried to say it—two years old.

There was something wrong with his tongue, something the matter
with the way he had to use his mouth, with the way his lips refused
to shape the words he meant to say.

He tried to define the words, tried to tell himself what he meant by
two years old and one moment it seemed that he knew the meaning
of it and then it escaped him.

The bat came again and he huddled close against the ground,
shivering as he crouched. He lifted his eyes fearfully, darting glances
here and there, and out of the corner of his eye he saw the looming
house and it was a place he knew as refuge.

"House," he said, and the word was wrong, not the word itself, but
the way he said it.

He ran on trembling, unsure feet and the great door loomed before
him, with the latch too high to reach. But there was another way, a
small swinging door built into the big door, the sort of door that is
built for cats and dogs and sometimes little children. He darted

through it and felt the sureness and the comfort of the house about him. The sureness and the comfort—and the loneliness.

He found his second-best teddy bear, and, picking it up, clutched it to his breast, sobbing into its scratchy back in pure relief from terror.

There is something wrong, he thought. Something dreadfully wrong. Something is as it should not be. It is not the garden or the darkened bushes or the swooping winged shape that came out of the night. It is something else, something missing, something that should be here and isn't.

Clutching the teddy bear, he sat rigid and tried desperately to drive his mind back along the way that would tell him what was wrong. There was an answer, he was sure of that. There was an answer somewhere; at one time he had known it. At one time he had recognized the need he felt and there had been no way to supply it—and now he couldn't even know the need, could feel it, but he could not know it.

He clutched the bear closer and huddled in the darkness, watching the moonbeam that came through a window, high above his head, and etched a square of floor in brightness.

Fascinated, he watched the moonbeam and all at once the terror faded. He dropped the bear and crawled on hands and knees, stalking the moonbeam. It did not try to get away and he reached its edge and thrust his hands into it and laughed with glee when his hands were painted by the light coming through the window.

He lifted his face and stared up at the blackness and saw the white globe of the Moon, looking at him, watching him. The Moon seemed to wink at him and he chortled joyfully.

Behind him a door creaked open and he turned clumsily around.

Someone stood in the doorway, almost filling it—a beautiful person who smiled at him. Even in the darkness he could sense the sweetness of the smile, the glory of her golden hair.

"Time to eat, Andy," said the woman. "Eat and get a bath and then to bed."

Andrew Young hopped joyfully on both feet, arms held out—happy and excited and contented.

"Mummy!" he cried. "Mummy ... Moon!"

He swung about with a pointing finger and the woman came swiftly across the floor, knelt and put her arms around him, held him close against her. His cheek against hers, he stared up at the Moon and it was a wondrous thing, a bright and golden thing, a wonder that was shining new and fresh.

\*

On the street outside, Stanford and Riggs stood looking up at the huge house that towered above the trees.

"She's in there now," said Stanford. "Everything's quiet so it must be all right."

Riggs said, "He was crying in the garden. He ran in terror for the house. He stopped crying about the time she must have come in."

Stanford nodded. "I was afraid we were putting it off too long, but I don't see now how we could have done it sooner. Any outside interference would have shattered the thing he tried to do. He had to really need her. Well, it's all right now. The timing was just about perfect."

"You're sure, Stanford?"

"Sure? Certainly I am sure. We created the android and we trained her. We instilled a deep maternal sense into her personality. She knows what to do. She is almost human. She is as close as we could come to a human mother eighteen feet tall. We don't know what Young's mother looked like, but chances are he doesn't either. Over the years his memory has idealized her. That's what we did. We made an ideal mother."

"If it only works," said Riggs.

"It will work," said Stanford, confidently. "Despite the shortcomings we may discover by trial and error, it will work. He's

# SECOND CHILDHOOD

been fighting himself all this time. Now he can quit fighting and shift responsibility. It's enough to get him over the final hump, to place him safely and securely in the second childhood that he had to have. Now he can curl up, contented. There is someone to look after him and think for him and take care of him. He'll probably go back just a little further ... a little closer to the cradle. And that is good, for the further he goes, the more memories are erased."

"And then?" asked Riggs worriedly.

"Then he can proceed to grow up again."

They stood watching, silently.

In the enormous house, lights came on in the kitchen and the windows gleamed with a homey brightness.

I, too, Stanford was thinking. Some day, I, too. Young has pointed the way, he has blazed the path. He had shown us, all the other billions of us, here on Earth and all over the Galaxy, the way it can be done. There will be others and for them there will be more help. We'll know then how to do it better.

Now we have something to work on.

Another thousand years or so, he thought, and I will go back, too. Back to the cradle and the dreams of childhood and the safe security of a mother's arms.

It didn't frighten him in the least.

www.ingramcontent.com/pod-product-compliance
Lightning Source LLC
Chambersburg PA
CBHW021006150626
46549CB00012BA/1382